BIKER'S REJECTED TRIPLETS

BWWM Mafia Romance

Jolie Damman

CONTENTS

Title Page

Copyright

Chapter 1   1

Chapter 2   4

Chapter 3   8

Chapter 4   11

Chapter 5   14

Chapter 6   17

Chapter 7   20

Chapter 8   24

Chapter 9   28

Chapter 10   31

Chapter 11   34

Chapter 12   38

Chapter 13   42

Chapter 14   45

Chapter 15   49

Chapter 16   53

Zhaire's Epilogue   56

Larry's Epilogue   59

Teaser: Biker's Secret Twins   63

Similar Books 67

About the Author 69

CHAPTER 1

Zhaire

I was running down the street, running for my life. I just didn't want to spend any other second with my fiancé. He was the worst man that ever showed up in my life. I hated him. He hated me, and he was using this opportunity to take advantage of me. To destroy my life more than it already was.

That was why I was running down the street and that was why I wasn't even looking back. The street was dark. I couldn't see anything, but I could see enough. I could see what was in front of me. I could see that I was heading somewhere, perhaps where I could feel safe and feel like I had some control over what was happening.

After what he told me, the last thing I wanted was to head back home.

I wasn't going to. No matter how poor I was, I wasn't going to return to my old life.

He almost hit me tonight, and that was something I could never forgive or forget.

My wrist was in pain. I could still feel like his hand was gripping it, his fingers digging deep into the skin, and that wasn't even the beginning of everything that happened tonight.

He wanted me tonight in his home. I didn't have to, but I went there anyway. Why did I do that? It was pretty obvious. Since I was still obviously going to get married to him, I decided to do something that was taught to me a long time ago. When I was still a kid…

When I was still a kid, my mother told me that I always had to give the people I didn't like a chance. So that was what I did, and now I hated myself for it. I hated myself for it because deep inside my heart I knew that I was going to find myself in this situation, running for my life.

But the thing about this was that my fiancé wasn't even coming after me. I thought that he was going to let the dogs chase after me, to destroy me, but that wasn't what was happening. I couldn't hear any dogs coming in this direction, which was relieving.

But it still didn't mean anything. My fiancé knew that I eventually would have to go back home. After all, I had told my father everything – everything he wanted to hear, that was. I told him that I was going to have a happy life with my husband. I told him that because I didn't want to disappoint him. He was a good man and he didn't deserve to think and worry that my life with my fiancé was going to be a living hell.

And it was always going to be that way. I remembered him from high school. There had been an incident, and he had – and was still thinking that – I was the one that caused his mother's car accident. He still hated me for it.

Now, he was someone important. Or at least, he thought he was important. He was always way over his head, thinking that everyone should suck up to him, but not me, and not anyone that ever had some self-respect.

Tonight, he had shouted at my face. He had shouted so many horrible things about me, dissing me, criticizing everything that my father ever did, and that wasn't even the beginning of everything I had to hear before I decided to bolt out of the house.

To be honest, I was just happy and content that he hadn't sent his guards after me. I was sure that he could have done that, and it would have been so easy for his guards to capture me.

I was running down the street and I had no idea when I would finally stop. It was only when I reached a park surrounded by tall buildings that I realized I couldn't keep this up much longer.

I put my hands on my knees, stopping what I was doing, and I was huffing, my heart still speeding up. Even though I had been running this whole time, my body just wasn't for this kind of thing. I didn't like to admit it, but I wanted to lose some weight, even though I was pretty much – mostly – content with my body.

Eventually, I took a deep breath in, realizing that the park was mostly silent and so quiet that I could still hear my own breathing. That wasn't something that happened often. Where I lived, it was always noisy, and it felt so weird to be in a place where silence ruled.

I thought I was going to get mugged in here or that perhaps something even worse was going to happen, but so far, that hadn't been the case. I looked around me, and I realized that I was almost in the middle of the park. Thankfully, it wasn't big or too spacious. It was actually quite small.

I didn't know which park this was. I didn't even know this part of the city well. When it came down to it, I just refused to come here often, and the reason for that was pretty obvious. This part of the city sucked. I could feel the fakeness, the lies, the hypocrisy, and everything else in the air.

It was quite funny, thinking about it. Whenever a place got too rich, all of that always happened. It always lost all the culture, the people that made it what it was, the history, and everything was replaced by what was the blandest of everything. Just thinking about it, I hated it.

When my breathing was finally returning to normal, I started to step toward the edge of the park and as far away from my fiancé's house as I could. Tonight, things were going to be different. I was already promising myself that much, and that I was going to tell my father everything. I was going to rat out my fiancé.

I was going to destroy his life just like he was destroying mine.

And I could never, and I would never think that being in a relationship was a good thing. There was no love.

CHAPTER 2

Larry

I figured something wrong was going on the moment when I noticed that that woman was running down the street and then entered the park where I was with my mates. She was now stepping toward us, and the moment when her eyes noticed that I was here too, she turned around.

I knew who she was. Zhaire Evans. One of the most striking women that ever walked in the world, and just looking at her, I wanted to be with my hands all over her body.

But I couldn't and I shouldn't do that, especially because the president of the Burnt Rodents was with me. He was the new president after the fiasco with Fred. I didn't know the full details of what happened, but I knew enough. I knew that he almost destroyed the motorcycle club, and that was something we could never forget or forgive.

He ran away with his wife. That was pretty much the only thing we could feel some comfort on. At least he found the person that he wanted to spend the rest of his life with.

But that wasn't enough, and soon we would find him. Soon we would find him and we would destroy him. But for the time being, we had something more important in our minds, and that was reestablishing the motorcycle club to its old glories.

Could we do that? We didn't know, but we weren't actually thinking about that right now.

I couldn't speak for my mates, but I knew we were all thinking about what our eyes were seeing. That lonely, single woman perambulating in the park, for the time being looking like she didn't even know where she was going.

Zhaire… What the hell happened? I asked myself, remembering that we had something in common. Something important, something that couldn't be erased.

We were both going to get married, only that we were going to do that with different people, and it sucked. I didn't want to get married to my old lady. That's what we called our girlfriends in the motorcycle club 'niche,' and it was one of the many things about it that I hated.

But I was poor, I didn't have much going on in my life, and I didn't have any prospect of ever finding something better and more interesting for it. I would like to work in a company, to be useful, to do something that didn't mean I was running from the police all the time, but that was something for another time, for when I thought that I could one day believe that I could turn my life around.

"Hey, are you seeing this?" The president of the club asked, making me remember how much I hated him, especially for the way that he forced me into my current marriage.

He thought I was his second-in-command. The second most important member of the motorcycle club, the one that people looked up to when things were going from bad to worse, and when he wasn't around.

"Yeah, I'm seeing it. She's Zhaire, an old friend of mine, and someone who hates me more than anyone else," I said, getting off my motorcycle. We were hanging out right around the edge of the park, just smoking, drinking, and talking about our lives, all the while checking every corner for any police officers that might come here.

So far, we were lucky with that.

"Hey, pretty girl, what do you think you are doing in the middle of this park and at night?" The president asked, making me wince. That was the last thing I needed. He didn't know Zhaire, of course.

He knew that I knew her, and that was enough for him. When he was thinking about something, when he was starting to get obsessed with it, he did things that he couldn't even regret later, and I was beginning to think that this was one of them.

I sighed, running my hand over my face. He got off the motorcycle and started to strut over to Zhaire, who for the time being was walking away from us with hurried footsteps.

She hated me.

She hated me because of the person I turned out to be when I was older and when we left high school. When she realized that I was walking down this path to become a biker, she couldn't be with me anymore.

When we were growing up, there was a spark between us, but now it was lost, and I didn't think it could ever be recovered.

"Hey, wait up, pretty girl. Are you lost? Are you looking for support? Did your man hurt you?" The president asked again, and the only thing I wanted to do right now was to punch his face so hard that his teeth would come flying out, but I wasn't going to do that. This wasn't the first time that he was singling someone out.

I just hated that he was doing it to my crush, and even more than that, that I had to keep pretending that everything was fine and dandy with this. It wasn't. I could feel my blood boiling.

Zhaire, in the meantime, wasn't at all interested. She just kept on striding away from us as quickly as she could, and then she reached the end of the park. The other end of it, far away from where we were on our motorcycles before.

When she was there, she looked from side to side, and even though I hated this moment for everything that it entailed, I still couldn't help but feel my cock getting harder in my pants.

This was far from a romantic and erotic moment at night, but I still couldn't help but feel that way, and it was kind of infuriating.

Just when we were stepping closer to her, we realized that we weren't alone. The police had come. Tires screeching, blasting sirens, and someone else was with them.

Someone that I should know. Someone that I knew. Someone

that I hated, and I was also feeling suspicious that this whole incident was happening because of him. He had to be the one behind it all.

He couldn't take his guards to come and do this. He had to call the police, and now we were in trouble.

Even the president and the rest of the motorcycle club started to shout, holler, running away in different directions only to go to their motorcycles the moment the police announced we were going to be locked up in jail.

And in the meantime, I couldn't move. I was frozen in place. That was happening to me because Zhaire was looking at me with pleading, beady eyes, and I was the only one that could help her right now.

Thus, without giving it a second thought, I just grabbed her hand and then sped away from there as quickly as I could with her, and without even thinking about my motorcycle.

Forget it. There was something much more important going on, and that was making sure that Zhaire was safe.

CHAPTER 3

Larry

Except that that wasn't going to be so easy. The police were on our tail, and we couldn't do much about that. They were coming after us. I could hear them behind us, and my heart was speeding up, feeling slightly afraid that they were going to lock us up.

But that wasn't going to happen. It wasn't the first time I was running away from the police, and it would never be the last.

I crossed the street with Zhaire and I knew that she had plenty of questions in her mind to ask me. But now was not the moment for that, and she knew that. She was coming with me without complaining about anything, and I just remembered that this was the first time in a very long time that we were seeing each other and that I was holding her hand. Just like in the good old times, when we were teenagers in high school and we were running away from her father, who despised me more than his own personal failures.

He hated me because he saw me for the person I was and for the person I was going to become even before it all happened.

We were running down an alleyway now, and then down another, and then one more. It was like a maze in here. Everything was massive, everything was big, it was all dark, and yet... I still knew where I was going.

Even though it was kind of overwhelming, I wasn't going to

get lost here.

Minutes later, I couldn't hear the police anymore. I mean, I could still hear them, but they were so far away from us, and even though they had maps, GPS, and everything they needed, they couldn't and would never be able to track us down here.

That was why I felt safe, and that was why Zhaire let go of my hand.

I turned around slowly, seeing her, and noticing how tired she was. The only thing I wanted to do right now was to take her in my arms and move away from here as quickly as I could with her, but I knew that she would never accept something like that. That was how she was.

She detested me, and I could see that just by looking at her face. She wanted nothing more than the worst for me.

"Larry, I don't know what you're thinking, but this doesn't mean anything."

After a moment of silence, I asked, "Are you going to tell me what you were doing running away from your fiancé?" I crossed my arms over my chest, tipping up my chin. "I thought that you were happy with him."

She scoffed. "You thought that I was happy with him?" She asked, crossing her arms over her chest and stepping away from me. "You really don't know anything about me. At high school, I thought you were someone I could trust, someone that could be with me, someone that I loved, and someone that understood me, but now I realize that it was all nothing more than a lie."

And the moment she finished saying that, I felt like she wanted to cry. I felt it in her voice. But she was stronger than that, and she was not going to do that.

After another moment of nothingness, with the police still searching for us in the alleyways, she asked, "And what about your fiancée, aren't you happy that you're going to marry her?"

Zhaire didn't want to admit it, but it was pretty obvious what she thought about it. She was salty about it. She had always wanted me, and now she thought that she had lost me for good.

I couldn't blame her for thinking that way.

"No, I don't really like her. I thought that was something I made obvious a long time ago, in a very similar moment, and when you had asked me about it as well, just like you're asking now."

She scoffed, whirling around and then thrusting her finger onto my chest. She wasn't crying, but her eyes were bloodshot, and I could see the way that her chest was expanding and contracting. This was all taking quite a toll on her.

"I trusted you. I thought you were everything to me. You are the first that kissed me. You said you loved me, and then you decided to throw your life away by joining the Burnt Rodents. I still have no idea what you thought you were doing. That was when my father crossed the line between us, and ever since then, we couldn't see each other anymore. I've... *missed* you."

I took a deep breath in. I didn't think we were going to start this discussion, especially when we still had to run away from the police. I mean, where we were was mostly safe, but they could still find us, and if that happened, I wouldn't be able to protect her.

I had my gun with me, though. It was in my waist and in case I needed it, I would use it, but for the time being, I was hoping that I wouldn't have to do that.

There was still so much that happened between us, so much that needed to be cleared, but I didn't think that we were going to have enough time for that, especially because someone had just entered the place where we were, and he had his gun pointed at me.

CHAPTER 4

Zhaire

The last thing I thought was going to happen was my fiancé finding me in this place. It was so hidden between the alleyways; a quiet, small, dark spot on a map, and, most likely, it didn't even exist on any map. But he had found us, and it was more than obvious that he wasn't going to let this slide.

He had a gun.

I was shocked. The last thing I thought I was going to learn about him was that he liked using guns, even though this moment was beyond anything I ever thought possible that could happen between us.

And he wasn't crying or showing any signs that this was affecting him more than it was affecting me.

"So, it looks like I finally found you," he said, putting his finger on the trigger, and for a moment I really thought that he was going to press it, but he didn't, which made me feel relieved. I let out a gush of air through my nostrils.

"Kenneth, what the hell do you think you're doing? You're going to hurt someone with that gun," I tried to warn, but he didn't even look in my direction. He had always treated me like I was a cockroach and now was no different.

He was smirking. I didn't know what he was thinking, but it was obvious that he was actually enjoying the moment. He was cherishing it.

"I have always been looking for that guy. I have always hated you, Larry, a.k.a. the 'Rescuer.'"

'Rescuer' was his biker nickname.

"What do you think you're doing, Kenneth?"

He looked at me with disdain in his eyes. "I'm here to do something I should have done a long time ago. Larry is the reason why you are not happy with me."

That came out of nowhere and I didn't know how to react. One moment he was turning my life into a living hell, throwing things at me, trying to make me feel miserable about everything I did, and now he was bothered that I wasn't happy with him?

Of course I wasn't going to be happy with him. He was the worst fiancé that could ever have shown up in my life.

"Larry doesn't have anything to do with me anymore. I ran into him by chance. That was all that happened," I tried to explain, but he shook his head, showing me that he wasn't going to believe any of my words.

And in the meantime, I was just hoping that Larry wasn't going to take out his gun as well and point it at my fiancé. That could end badly. It could end in a brief shootout with all of us dead, and I didn't even want to be thinking about that.

It made my skin crawl. It made my heart speed up.

I put myself between them. I knew I was crazy, but this moment was calling for something like that. Larry lifted his hand and then he almost reached for his gun. I thought he was going to do it, but when he realized that I didn't want to, he didn't.

That was one of the positives about him. When I didn't want him to do something, he didn't. He always respected me. The reasons why we didn't end up together were that my father didn't want it, and because I didn't want to be involved with those bikers, too.

"He has everything to do with this!" Kenneth shouted, showing me more and more how angry he was. I was worried about where this was going, where it was leading, but at this point, there was nothing else I could do about it other than to stand between them. I knew that Kenneth wasn't going to press the trigger as long as his gun was pointed at me.

"Just let it out, Kenneth. Let it all out and tell me everything you feel about me," Larry taunted, smiling. Why was he smiling? I asked myself, looking incredulous at him. That wasn't why this should be happening. It shouldn't be happening like this. He was already in danger and we knew that if a shot was fired, the police would swarm over here, putting us all in jail, and that was something we could not afford to let happen.

"I fucking hate you, you motherfucker. I hate you so fucking much. I hate you for everything that you've done against me, for destroying my life, and for stealing my fiancée. It all ends here and now," Kenneth spewed out, throwing his body to the right, re-aiming his gun, and then pressing the trigger. He was smarter than I thought, especially for someone that was so distressed.

I heard the shot blasting in the dark, and I jumped in the direction where it was going. I didn't know why I did that, only that I thought it was the right thing to do.

Larry didn't have anything to do with this. It was Kenneth that was paranoid about me and him, and he still thought that I had something to do with my high school sweetheart.

And then, I felt something sharp and small going inside my shoulder, and I collapsed on the floor, my knees weak all of a sudden.

I heard a shout, more gunshots, and then Kenneth falling on the floor, his gun skidding away from his hand.

I didn't know what was happening, but I felt so much pain in my entire body, and I was struggling to keep my eyes open.

Everything was getting dark. Was I dying? I didn't know, but it certainly felt like that…

CHAPTER 5

When I reopened my eyes, the next thing I thought was that all of this was weird. A moment later I was shot. My own fiancé had shot me, and I couldn't wrap my head around it.

My head… It was funny that I could still feel it, and it was funny that it hurt so much.

At least I was alive, I thought, looking around me and finding out that I was in a dark room. It was quite moldy, and I could smell the odor of cheap smoke in the air from even cheaper cigarettes. I didn't know what happened or was happening, for that matter, but I was still worried.

What was going on here? I asked myself, noticing that a blanket covered my body. Whoever had taken me here, obviously cared about the cold of the night. Even though it was the summer, here in this desert, which surrounded the city, the nights were always cold, and tonight was no different.

And yet, I still felt hot, like I had a fever. I didn't know if that was the case, but it certainly felt like that. Thinking that, I pushed the blanket off my body and tried to move my legs, but I soon realized that it wasn't just my head that hurt, but my entire body.

And just when I tried to do something else, I heard footsteps coming in this direction. I panicked. The first thing that crossed my mind was that someone was going to come here to kill me, perhaps to finish the job. I was exposed and vulnerable, after all.

My heart was speeding up, and I was so scared. I didn't think I had ever felt so scared in my life before.

And I didn't have anything to protect myself with. Not a gun and not even a knife.

Seconds later, I felt relieved. A man was standing in the doorway, and he was none other than Larry. He actually had something in his hand. It wasn't breakfast and it certainly wasn't good. It certainly wasn't something that I would eat in the morning, but I supposed that it was better than nothing.

"Morning," he said, his voice lacking emotion, stepping to me. He had seen that I was scared and that, the moment when my eyes noticed that it was him that was coming, I was relieved. "I brought... Something for you. I had to go out to the Burger King down the street quickly so that no one could identify me. They are looking for me. The police want to lock me up."

He gave me the box. It was a small box with a cheeseburger inside it. I didn't like it, but it really was better than nothing, and my stomach was also growling.

"Thanks," I said, my tone also lacking any emotion, opening the box and then taking out the cheeseburger. It was as oily and as fat as I remembered it the last time that I ate it, and that was a long time ago. I was trying to follow my diet, even though that was harder than I had thought.

"Are you, uh, feeling okay?" He asked while I took my first bite of the cheeseburger, munching it. I knew that I felt this just because I was hungry as fuck. In other circumstances, I would be hating this cheap, fat food.

But right now, the cheap bread and the burger actually felt good on my tongue, and thus I soon found myself munching the rest of the cheeseburger, and I knew I was going to eat it whole. "That bastard... He shot at you. I can never forgive him."

Now, he'd just made me remember everything that had happened. Kenneth had really pressed the trigger of his handgun, had shot me while aiming at Larry, and he was the one that he wanted to kill. I never thought that he felt so much anger for

Larry.

I nodded. I didn't feel exactly okay, but it was better than worrying him. Larry was capable of anything and everything when he was worried about me, and now would be no different. I just didn't want him to do anything stupid.

"Don't lie to me. I know that you tried to get out of bed but couldn't because of the pain."

I took another bite of the burger, now noticing that I had almost finished eating half of it.

He was always perceptive and now was no different.

"It hurts, I'm not going to lie, but I still feel okay. You don't need to worry about me. You need to worry about what happened over there."

I swallowed the lump in my throat. "What happened there? Did you kill him?" I added after that.

There was a moment of silence and it was unnerving. Was he going to answer my question? I didn't know. He was with his back leaning on the wall, his arms crossed over his chest, looking at nowhere in particular. I didn't even know where we were, but it was obvious that this place was safe for the time being.

Larry was the kind of man that knew everything about the city, all the spots, all the places where we could hide. It was like he had a map in his head.

"I shot at him, yeah, and I'm not going to lie. I hit his chest and then he fell to the ground, and I didn't have enough time to check his pulse or anything of the sort. The next moment, he was lying on the floor, and I just knew that I had to get you somewhere safe. So, I took you here, and now you are feeling slightly better. It's a good thing that I know a thing or two about how to remove a bullet from a person's shoulder."

CHAPTER 6

Zhaire

There was a moment of silence. "Even though I don't like to admit it, I have to say – thank you for saving me. Kenneth was crazy. He was unhinged. I didn't know what he was thinking, bringing a gun with him, but in the end... I think that you just saved me from him, and that is a lot more than I thought would ever happen between us."

Larry was still looking nowhere in particular, and then he uncrossed his arms, going out of the room. It had already been a couple of minutes since I started to eat the cheeseburger, and even though I didn't like the taste, it was still good.

The bad thing about it was that since it had little in terms of nutrition, I was probably going to feel hungry a couple of minutes from now.

Either way, I wasn't thinking about that right now. I was thinking about something else.

I was thinking about going to the bathroom. That was where I needed to go and where I was thinking about going before he appeared.

I hated to admit it, but I was going to need Larry's help with that.

"I don't take pleasure in what I did. I was just protecting myself and you."

I took a deep breath and said, "Does this place happen to have a bathroom? I need to go there." I bit my bottom lip. "I need to pee."

I felt heat rushing to my cheeks after saying that. It felt so odd saying those words, especially to someone that had been my boyfriend in high school.

"Sure, I can help you," he said, coming over, and then he let me put my arm around his shoulders, and I couldn't help but feel the wetness that started to form in my pussy.

It was involuntary and it was happening without my consent, but I still felt it. The thing was that ever since high school, Larry had really become a much more handsome man, and now it was the first time in years that I was feeling more than his hand. I was feeling my skin on his shoulders, how firm and hard his muscles were, and well… I wanted more of this.

But I knew I shouldn't. I knew how dangerous it was to let my feelings for Larry speak louder than the rational part of my mind.

"Come on, up you go," he said, taking me to the bathroom. He opened the door, and in the meantime, I tried to check if there was something on his face that showed me how he was feeling about this.

Did Larry still feel something for me? I didn't know. Part of me kind of hoped he did, but I knew I couldn't get my hopes up, thus I immediately squashed them.

My fiancé had hit my shoulder with the bullet, and yet my entire body hurt.

Larry opened the door of the bathroom, letting me inside. I supported my weight with my hand on the wall, and then I looked into his eyes. They weren't just the eyes of someone worried about what was going to happen from now on - he was concerned with something even more problematic than that.

Larry was worried about me.

That realization dawned on me, and I didn't know what to do with it.

"Thanks," I said briefly, closing the door of the bathroom, and then opening the lid of the toilet. I supposed I should be thankful that at least we had this bathroom, but the toilet and everything else in here was still nasty.

Just being in this bathroom, I didn't want to spend another minute in here, and I couldn't help but wonder if I could just walk out of this building and call my family, especially my father.

But I didn't want to do that because Larry had said he wasn't sure if Kenneth was alive or not. In case he was still alive, he would come for me. He would make sure that this time I would never be able to escape from his house, and that was a thought that scared me more than anything else did.

No, I really couldn't walk out of this building. Not without first waiting a little while and finding out what was going to happen in the coming days.

As for Larry… I was certain that he wasn't even thinking about going out. He had his biker friends, so he was going to be okay. All he did was kill a person, if Kenneth even died, that was.

He really could be alive.

Not wanting to think about that anymore, I sat down on the toilet, noticing that there was no toilet paper, so I couldn't cover the lid with some of it. My ass was going to touch the lid, and that thought disgusted me.

And yet, I still had to do it, so I sat down on the lid. I felt like puking, but at least I was peeing, thinking that this all felt so weird. I couldn't help but wonder what was going to happen next. Was I really going to have to spend a couple days here with Larry, a biker and a member of the 1%?

I didn't know, but thinking about it, I felt like breaking down, and I did. I buried my face in my hands, crying, sobbing, and I was just hoping that Larry couldn't hear any of that.

I didn't want him to worry. If there was something that he always did when he noticed that he was needed, it was to show his support and be nosey, and that was something I didn't need.

I sighed, stopping my crying and sobbing, and then I stood up after flushing the toilet. I washed my hands without hand soap, dried them on my pants, and after opening the door of the bathroom, I noticed that Larry was standing right in front of me.

He was going to be his nosey self again.

CHAPTER 7

The prospect of spending a couple of days here with my high school sweetheart was tempting, I wasn't going to lie. This whole time, I had been hating that my life was going in the direction it was going to, but now, thinking about this, it could be the change it needed.

I took a deep breath.

It was just like I had said before. Zhaire was still as stunning as ever, and she was looking at me with beady, bloodshot eyes. When I was crossing in front of the bathroom, I did hear that she was crying and sobbing.

The moment when I heard that, the first thought that crossed my mind was how much I wanted to help her. I remembered everything that happened between us, and how hurtful our breakup had been.

And now, she was here with me and we were stuck together. I had no idea how many days we were going to be spending here in this place, this dingy apartment in the middle of nowhere, but my mind couldn't stop thinking that it presented an opportunity.

An opportunity that I couldn't stop thinking about. I was obsessing over it.

"You didn't hear that, or did you?" She asked, taking a step back.

"I heard everything. I heard that you were crying. If there's something you want to tell me, then just do it. I know that you are going through a lot."

"Thank you for taking me here, but I'm already feeling a lot better," she said, pushing past me, but then she lost her balance and she was going to fall over if I wasn't more perceptive. The moment when I noticed that was happening, I threw my arms around her, and I felt the heat of her body on me.

I couldn't deny that I was hard.

I pulled Zhaire to me tighter just to make sure that she really wasn't going to fall on the floor. And she didn't, but that ended up leading to something that shouldn't be happening.

My cock ended up pressing against her ass, and as soon as that happened, I noticed her cheeks flushing. They were beet-red.

A moment later, Zhaire pushed herself away from me, and she only didn't fall on the floor this time because she supported her weight against the wall.

"That's why I said what I said before, last time we met. I don't want to be with you. I know that you want to take advantage of me, and I know exactly what's going on in your dirty mind."

I let her move away from me, stumbling. There was no point in being stubborn with her. That would only make her even more annoyed than she was.

And yet, Zhaire was in so much pain that she couldn't move anywhere without my help. Sure, she could stand where she was for as much time as she wanted, but to go back to her bedroom – which was the only bathroom in the apartment – she was going to need my help again.

So, that was why I was waiting where I was, with my hands in my pockets.

She tried to take a step forward. Damn, Zhaire really could be so stubborn sometimes. She learned from the best, I thought, remembering her father and everything he had said to me when I was still in high school.

I despised him so much, I thought, thinking about nothing more than punching him until he was begging for my forgiveness.

"You are going to need my help to go to the bedroom," I said matter-of-factly.

"No, I really don't need your help with anything, and I'm getting out of this apartment right now," she affirmed, and this time she managed to take a couple steps forward, but then she grimaced, stopping where she was.

To be honest, I was surprised by her strength. She had always been strong, but the pain that she was feeling all through her body – it was really a lot.

After a moment of nothingness, I promised, "I promise that I'm not going to do anything you don't want. I'm only going to help you. You want to go to the bedroom, lie in the bed, close your eyes, fall asleep, and pretend that nothing of this is happening, and that's really all something you deserve. You are going through a lot, after all."

She bit her bottom lip, looking over her shoulder and at me. Was Zhaire really going to do something that wasn't so stubborn right now? I didn't know, but I was waiting where I was, and in the meantime, my mind couldn't stop thinking about how hot she was and how fast my heart was beating.

"Fine, but the moment you touch a part of me that you shouldn't, I'm going to punch you so hard that you are going to regret it."

I smirked. I knew she was going to say something like that, and I wasn't surprised by it. I let Zhaire put her arm around my shoulders again and then I took her to the bedroom, making sure that my dick wasn't getting any harder than it already was.

Again, I didn't want her to notice my boner. And she didn't, thank goodness. I helped her lie down in the bed and then she pulled up the comforter, turning around so that she wasn't looking at me.

Zhaire still despised me so much, and I could do nothing to change that.

I walked over to the door, closed it, and then I gave her one last, long glance, thinking about how angelic she looked now that she was lying in the bed.

I just hoped that everything was going to be okay and that she was going to sleep well.

There were going to be so many things to fix in the coming hours and days, after all.

CHAPTER 8

Zhaire

I opened my eyes and found myself in a completely different place. Where was I? I asked myself, checking my surroundings and in a moment, everything became clear to me. I knew this place. I'd been here so many times.

This was my fiancé's house. What happened? I asked myself, realizing that I was in his living room, to be more precise.

I didn't know what was going on in here. One moment I was in that dingy apartment, trying to keep everything together, and now I was here. I was at my fiancé's house, and I just wanted to get out of here as soon as possible.

The fact that I was here meant that he was alive. Alive and kicking. He was going to show up soon enough, find me here, and then all the torture was going to start happening again.

I couldn't let that happen. I wasn't going to, no matter how much I hated Larry. He was the only one that knew how I felt about this, and I knew that he was going to help me.

I took a deep breath, whirling around, and then bolting to the door out of the house. I was going to get there. I was going to escape again, or at least that was what I was thinking when I felt a hand clamping around my neck and then yanking me back with all of his strength.

Kenneth's strength, I soon realized when I fell on my ass and he was standing on top of me. He was staring down at me with hatred in his eyes, and I knew he was thinking about just one thing – killing me.

And yet, not before torturing me as much as he could, too.

I tried to scream and shriek, but I couldn't. It was like there was something in my mouth and around it, closing it, and as much as I tried, I couldn't even move my lips.

I didn't know what was happening, but I just wanted it all to end. It had to. This had to be a nightmare.

"Zhaire, wake up!" Someone shouted from far away, but his voice was getting closer. Wait, that voice... I knew whose voice that was. Larry. He was coming here and he was going to help me.

He was the only one that could. The only one strong enough to stand up to Kenneth, who wasn't someone even that important that he could pose much danger to anyone.

And then, everything became clear, and yet everything around me was still dark.

I was back in the old apartment with Larry. He was sitting on the bed where I was lying, and he was looking at me with concerned eyes. They were wide.

He was shaking me with his hands on my shoulders and I felt how firm his grip on them was. I felt how calloused his fingers were, and I could feel a slight sense of arousal in me, which was something I really shouldn't be feeling.

"You were having a nightmare," he said matter-of-factly, taking his hands off me when he realized that I was getting back to this moment and that I had finally woken up from my nightmare.

I was breathing hard and it was hard to think about what was really going on.

Even though I had said before that I didn't even want him to touch me anywhere, I kind of missed feeling his hands on me. On my shoulders.

After a moment of silence, Larry asked, "Feeling better already?"

I checked his eyes and there was no denying that his question was genuine. He was indeed worried about me, and that was a lot more than Kenneth had ever shown to me.

"Yeah, I am. Thanks," I replied and I couldn't believe that I had just said that to him. I should never have said it. I should never have told him that I was thankful that he was here and supporting me after my nightmare.

And why was he even doing that? It wasn't like I was supporting him back or showing him that I really was thankful that he was here with me.

I just really missed his hands on my shoulders.

"Do you want to tell me what you were dreaming about?" He asked, and I shook my head.

Like hell I was going to tell him what I was dreaming about.

He took a deep sigh, standing up. "Well, if you change your mind, you know that I'm going to be here and that you are also going to be here for the next couple of days. I don't think that we are going anywhere for the time being."

That was a punch to my gut, but I couldn't deny that there was a positive about being here for a couple of days with him.

Just when he was going to the door, I asked, "And what about your fiancé? Does she know about what's happening here?" I asked, remembering that he was also going to get married.

I didn't even know his fiancée, not that it mattered much anyway.

I didn't have anything to do with her and I didn't want to, anyway.

"She knows about this, yeah, but I don't think that she's waiting for me. The truth is that... We don't really gel well together."

I widened my eyes.

I thought that they were going to have a great marriage, that it was going to be worth it, that it was going to be much better than the wedding I was going to have with Kenneth, but now that he had just said that... I didn't know anything anymore.

That was why I was blushing.

"Well, you sleep well. It's still early in the night," he said and then he closed the door.

Lying back down in the bed, I felt scared about going back

to sleep, but now that I knew he was here and listening to everything, I felt safe, despite not wanting that.

CHAPTER 9

Zhaire

It was the next morning and surprisingly the sun stood proud in the sky, the blueness of it catching the attention of my eyes, and I could see some sparse clouds in the distance. Some birds were even chirping in the trees, and I could feel the smell of flowers in the air, something that I had already grown unaccustomed to.

After living for so long thinking that my life with Kenneth was going to be a living hell – and for sure, it was going to be – I had begun to forget what flowers smelled like.

Was that different now because I was with my former high school sweetheart?

It couldn't be. We hadn't spent much time together yet and in the little time that we had together, we didn't really talk about each other much.

I had hoped that this was nothing more than a nightmare, too. But I was really here and this was really happening.

The first thought that crossed my mind was that I needed to ask Larry if he thought we could finally leave this place. But I knew that that was probably not going to be the answer. The reason for that was pretty simple. He was the kind of person that was always meticulous about everything, and now was going to be no different.

I stood up, went to the bathroom, took a quick shower, and

then I stepped out and I noticed that there was music playing in the background. It was a guitar. The music was nice and for the first time in a very long time, I also found myself enjoying it, frozen where I was, not doing anything else.

And I had really thought that it was a neighbor upstairs that was playing the guitar, but that wasn't the case. The music was actually coming from this apartment specifically, and that meant the person that was playing the guitar was none other than Larry himself.

For a moment, I was stunned. I remembered moments like this from high school, when he was sitting on a bench on campus, with his guitar propped on his lap, his fingers moving over strings, and playing his songs for hours on end, going as far as skipping some classes just so that he could train a little more.

What was even happening here? I asked myself, proceeding to the other side of the apartment, where the kitchen was. He was there. Larry was sitting on a stool and a guitar was on his lap, and he was playing it, his fingers moving over the strings.

This took me back. This took me back to high school, and for a moment, I could see his former self. I could see the person that I had fallen in love with, even though things were dire right now.

He hadn't realized that I was here, that I had already woken up. He was still playing the guitar, and I could tell that he hadn't done that in a long time.

I took a step forward and then he finally lifted his head, finding me. "I didn't realize you had already woken up."

"I didn't realize that you had a guitar with you," I said and his eyes shifted down, finding the guitar on his lap.

"Yeah, I guess I got lucky. I checked around this place a little and found this guitar. It's actually the same guitar that I had with me back in high school. I thought that someone had already stolen it," he said.

"Well, keep playing it a little while longer. I was actually enjoying that song you were playing."

"Really?" He asked, adjusting the guitar on his lap. "I couldn't really remember what it was like. It's one of the songs that I used to play back in school."

I pulled a stool over, sitting on it. "It was still good, though. I want to hear more of it, especially because it looks like we aren't going to be able to leave here soon, right?" I asked.

He sighed heavily.

"I did check the surroundings a little bit before and it's just as you say. The police are still looking for us and this is the best place to stay holed up, no doubt about it."

I shook my head, just finding it fortunate that I felt better and that I didn't feel as much pain as before.

"I suppose that is just the way it is."

When I was with my hands on my lap, he started playing the guitar again, and more and more I could see his old self. The one that I had fallen in love with.

Could it really be possible? Could he still be the same man? I didn't know, but the more I thought about it, the more time I wanted it to happen. I just didn't think it ever would, though it was nice that there was this thing connecting us now.

When he was done playing the song, he asked, looking up and I couldn't help but think that, deep inside him, he looked like a better, more composed version of his former self.

"Did you like it?" Larry queried, adjusting his guitar on his lap.

I blinked twice. It was like his question had taken me by surprise, and that… Really was the case.

It entranced me. It had done that and a lot more.

"Yeah, it was really good. Just like in high school."

CHAPTER 10

Larry

I t had been by accident more than anything that I had found this guitar in the apartment. The fact that she liked the song I had played for her was cool as well and also something I didn't expect.

After what happened last night, I was really thinking that she despised me so much she couldn't even enjoy a good song. Thankfully, that wasn't the case, and I could see some of the connection we had forming between us again.

Still, I was certain it would never happen.

I was walking in front of the only bedroom in the place when I heard her crying. For a moment, I couldn't notice it, but it was like my ears were attuned to it, and suddenly I found myself wishing to do something about it.

After all, everything that happened between us back in high school was still fresh in my mind.

This time, I was much more cautious about how I was approaching this. I knocked on her door and I didn't hear anything. I thought that Zhaire was going to say something, that she was busy with something else and didn't want to see me, but that wasn't the case.

Silence still filled the void between us.

I knocked on the door again and this time she said, "Larry? I'm doing something here and I can't lose my focus. It's important."

Zhaire was doing something? That was bullshit and I didn't even have to check it more closely to know that it just wasn't true.

"What's going on, Zhaire? I told you that you can tell me everything that is bothering you."

"Nothing is bothering me. Don't worry about me. Don't think that just because I listened to you playing a song on the guitar that we are lovers again."

Wow. I didn't think she was just going to straight up shoot those words at me. Was Zhaire really that pissed?

No, I shook my head, dismissing that worry. It couldn't be that.

She wasn't pissed at me that much. Something else was going on, and even though she was possibly going to hate me for this, I just needed to do it.

So, I opened the door and slowly, I stepped inside the room and… There Zhaire was, sitting on the bed, crying.

What I had thought before wasn't wrong. Zhaire really was crying, and seeing that broke my heart. I needed to do something about it, and not because I wanted to become her boyfriend again, but because it was the right thing to do. If there was something I hated seeing, it was a woman crying.

"I thought I told you not to open the door!" She barked, making me take a step back and if I had taken another, I would have really made the worst mistake I could have made here and now.

"You didn't tell me that."

She blinked twice. I was treading on dangerous territory, but I didn't care about it. The only thing I actually cared about was making sure that she wasn't going to do something so bad that it would leave her depressed.

"Well, it doesn't change anything. Just get out of the room. I don't need someone trying to find out everything I'm doing," she barked, turning so that her back was turned to me.

I took a couple steps forward. If she wanted me gone, she was going to have to try harder than that, I thought.

I sat on the bed by her side.

I shouldn't even be doing this, acting all worried, but the truth was that I was, and I still had so many good memories about what we had together back in high school.

Slowly but surely, Zhaire turned her head around, finding me. She tried to hit me with her hand, but she was no good doing that and it wasn't really a real attempt to get me away from here, anyway.

"What's going on? Why are you crying?" I asked and this time she completely broke down in front of me. Zhaire started to cry, sob, whimper, and the only thing I could do was to wrap her in my arms, which I immediately did, and I felt much better for it.

I let her cry on my chest and it appeared to be going on forever.

Zhaire pulled her head back and then her body. I wasn't going to lie. I was actually missing it already even though I wasn't able to 'feel' it as I normally would. Zhaire was still so stunning. It was like she didn't change at all since high school.

"I think that this is all too much for me. It's taking a toll on me, and I hate it. I want to get out of here, I want to get out of this shitty apartment, and I just want to stop thinking that there's still something between us."

I widened my eyes.

I never thought that Zhaire was thinking the same thing as well. She was also suspicious that we felt something strong for each other.

I wanted to reach over, cup her cheek in my hand, and kiss her, but I didn't know if I wanted the possible ramifications that would come after that.

"I'm going to do something about this. I'm going to get us out of here, and I'm going to make sure that the police never look for us again," I promised, putting my hand on her cheek, feeling how soft and smooth it was.

I stroked it. It felt right to be doing that and, truly, I didn't think I wanted to be doing anything different right now.

Then, I felt her leaning toward me, her eyes looking into mine, and I couldn't help but wonder what exactly she was thinking.

But it was like Zhaire wanted me to know what that was. She kissed me. Our lips connected, and it was like all the hatred between us didn't exist anymore.

CHAPTER 11

Larry

But it was like Zhaire wanted me to know what that was. She kissed me. Our lips connected, and it was like all the hatred between us didn't exist anymore.

It was all there, but it disappeared in an instant as we both melted into each other, kissing with a tenderness that left us breathless.

She leaned back, resting her forehead against mine, and her breath fanned my lips. My hands went to her waist, pulling her closer to me. This felt right too. I felt that we had always fit perfectly together.

She looked at me, caressing the tip of my nose with hers, before closing the distance between our bodies once again. And one more time, she kissed me.

This time, though, our kisses became deeper. Zhaire bit my lip slightly, and I let her. It made me feel dizzy.

When we parted again, I rested my forehead against hers, breathing heavily, and Zhaire smiled, her eyes closed.

"That...wasn't what I expected. But I'm glad it happened anyway."

"Me too. I wish things would have been easier between us."

Zhaire laughed softly at my answer, and for a few seconds, nothing mattered except the fact that I was here with her and it didn't seem like we would ever be able to leave.

"I'm so glad this is happening again," I said, stroking her cheek, putting my fingers under her shirt, and wondering how she felt about that. I checked her eyes to make sure I wasn't doing something stupid.

And she gave me the permission I was seeking.

She chuckled. "You know, I shouldn't really be doing this." And after hearing that, I pressed my finger to her lips.

"Don't say anything. You don't have to say anything to me," I affirmed, kissing her lips again and making sure that my lips lingered on hers a little while longer this time. She liked that. There was no denying it. I could see it in the way that her eyes glistened with deep, intense arousal.

Then, I pushed her body so that she was lying on the bed and I was on top of her. After I took off her shirt, my eyes scanned her body, and seeing what I was seeing wasn't enough. I needed more, and I was going to get more.

This was happening just like it happened in high school, but back then we had been cut short. That had been when her father had found out about it, confirming his suspicions about us. He had caused quite a scene, something that happened in the past. But that was it. It all happened in the past, and the now was the now. That was all that mattered.

Her skin was just so soft, and I loved it.

I didn't stop myself, lowering her pants and then thinking how wrong it was that she didn't have another pair. She needed another. In fact, Zhaire needed as much money as she could have so that she could buy all the clothes she wanted, and that was putting it mildly. That was how much I wanted her.

Zhaire arched her back when I put my hand on it, letting out a cloud of breath through her lips. Not being able to resist them again, I kissed her once more, making sure that my tongue went inside her mouth, battling against hers.

It was absolutely devastating the way that she started to grind her body against me, and even though this was barely the start of it, she was already sweating.

It was becoming more difficult to move my hands around her

body, but I was still holding her tightly to me, and now that she wore nothing more than her bra and pair of panties, I wanted something else.

"Do you want me to do this?" I asked, kissing her neck, making my way down to her breasts, my fingers looking for the hook of her bra. And whether she was going to say what I wanted or not, I was still going to do it.

"Yes," she purred, her hands moving around my body, feeling my muscles and cherishing them.

After hearing her words, the next thing I did was unhook her bra, tossing it aside. It was on the floor now and where it couldn't bother us. I turned my head back around, checking out the exposed torso that was under me, and it was absolutely breathtaking.

For a moment, it was like I was seeing it for the first time, but it wasn't.

And I couldn't help but wonder if, during this whole time, she had been taken by another man or not. I guessed that she could see the question in my eyes, for she quickly answered, "This is my first time, Larry."

My throat went dry all of a sudden. I figured she was going to say something impactful, but I didn't suspect that it was going to be so ground-shaking. If before I was hard, now I was even more so, and I could feel my cock finishing somersaults under my pants.

Fuck. She really was still a virgin? I couldn't believe it, I contemplated.

"Don't worry, Zhaire. I'm going to be careful with you," I promised, sliding my hands over her body, cupping her right breast with my itchy fingers and then easing her nipple between my lips, ascertaining myself that I was doing this as slowly and as painfully as possible without torturing her much.

The moment when my lips were applying pressure around her nipple, she bucked her hips, throwing her body against me, and I could feel the way that she was looking for my cock.

Well, since she wanted it so much, I was going to make sure that she was going to get it, I thought, taking off my belt and then tossing it aside. It fell on the floor with a light click of the locking mechanism. And then, I felt her hand seeking, craving my bulge.

She was really looking for it and it wasn't surprising when she finally enveloped it with her fingers, giving me everything I lusted after.

I didn't even have a condom with me. Being honest, the last thing I thought was that I was going to have sex these days. Things were dire between me and my fiancée, and I couldn't just fuck anyone else even though I wanted to, badly. I had promised the president of the Burnt Rodents that I was going to marry her and that we were going to have an amazing life together, but that didn't turn out to be the case.

Now... Now it was time for something else.

CHAPTER 12

Zhaire

Larry was on top of me, his body moving like a snake. His nickname was the 'Rescuer' and it was fitting for his burning presence. He was rescuing me right now, his hands swirling around my body, and this time he was also sucking on my right nipple, his tongue running on it, making sure that I was moaning and groaning loudly.

"Fuck, you're so hot," he cooed, pulling his head back, and a line of his drool formed between his lips and my tit. He flicked his finger on it while I started to pump his cock. It was massive – just as big as I remembered it – and I felt so much lust, my lips dry like sand.

I loved the way that he was sucking and swirling his tongue on my nipple, but even that wasn't enough, and I craved something else. Without giving it a second thought, I pushed him with my hands so that he was lying on the bed as well, and this time I was on top of him.

"Whoa," Larry muttered, his hands cupping my asscheeks and I felt his fingers digging into my skin. "Calm down. We have all the time in the world."

I chuckled, gliding my hands over his pecs and abs, cherishing how hard his muscles tensed under my sensitive touch.

"I think that we are past that," I joked, flicking my tongue out and then pulling myself down so that I was where I wanted. His dick was already out of his underwear and it was pointed at me.

It was obvious that Larry didn't like that he couldn't be cherishing my asscheeks with his hands any longer, but he didn't say anything about that, and he gave me all the time I required, bending my body until I was with my lips around his cockhead, and it was mouthwatering.

I swirled my tongue around it, making sure that I was focusing on all the pressure points, where he was most vulnerable, and he couldn't help but throw his head back into the mattress, letting me do everything I craved.

His pre-cum coated my tongue, and I cherished its saltiness. I just couldn't get enough of it. The more that I worked his prick, the bigger he appeared to grow, and I wanted to know what his limit was.

My tongue slid and played with his dickhead for what felt like hours, and I knew that he was close to cumming, though I wasn't going to let him – not yet, anyway. With that consideration in mind, I pressed the underside of his dickhead with my fingers, forcing him to reopen his eyes, and he did.

"What's going on, Zhaire?" He queried, and I knew that this was a mistake, but I still wanted to go along with it. The truth was that I wasn't on birth control, so whatever had to happen here, I knew that I wanted it and there was no point in even trying to stop it.

My life was fucked anyway. I might as well do something crazy for once. Considering that not much was working out for me, I didn't think there was an issue with that, and I was tired of all this shit anyway. I might as well do the one single thing that my heart was begging me to.

I positioned myself on top of him, lining up my pussy to his prick, and then I lowered my ass, making sure that he penetrated me. Larry gasped, but he still positioned his hands under my ass, digging his fingers into my skin.

"Do you really want to go on from here?" He asked and I noticed the dryness on his pink lips. I nodded. There was nothing else that I wanted to do more right now. Everything that I suppressed about us, our relationship, our everything came tumbling out, and I couldn't control any of that anymore.

I just wanted this rough, obsessed biker inside of me, deeper, fucking me, finally taking my virginity, and the gleam on his eyes told me that he thought the same. Our minds were almost intertwined.

"I like the way you think," he purred, his tone dry, and then he wasted no time, bouncing me up and down on his rod with his calloused hands, making sure that I was feeling as much pain as possible and without hurting me.

He popped my hymen and I squealed, throwing my head around, my hair flowing around us. It was messy, but I loved it.

This couldn't get any better.

I knew it was a mistake, but it was a mistake that I was happily making. Larry wasted no time, still thrusting against my ass, pounding in and out of me, and then suddenly everything got out of control, and he came inside of me.

Hot, creamy spurt after spurt of his cum, he filled me with his seed, and even though it was just a passing thought, I knew that I was going to get pregnant. I knew that the time was right, and if there was something that could finally make Kenneth stop thinking about me, it was that.

The moment he learned that I wasn't pure anymore, he would stop coming after me and would leave me alone. At least, that was what I was hoping for, I thought, coming at the same time as Larry did, his dick shooting out a couple more lines of his seed inside of me before, finally, he was empty.

I was huffing, breathing was difficult, and sweat covered my body, but this was still fulfilling, and I didn't want it to end, and yet… It wasn't like things could go that way.

I did what I had to, falling down onto the bed by his side, and then I felt him wrap his arms around me.

And just before I fell asleep, he murmured into my ear, "It doesn't matter what happened before now – I'm going to make sure that you are going to be safe and without Kenneth coming after you, if he still lives."

And I knew he promised me something he was going to uphold.

That was why I had such a huge smile on my face.

CHAPTER 13

Zhaire

I had woken up the next morning feeling satisfied, my hands and my arms looking for his body, but they found nothing. What? I asked myself, in a moment concluding that it was nothing to worry about. Chances were that Larry had gone to the kitchen, not that there was much of a kitchen in this apartment, though.

My hands fumbled with the bedsheets, looking for traces of his body, but I couldn't find anything. It was like Larry had never been here, which was silly, I thought, pushing myself up so that I was sitting on the bed.

I checked my surroundings, looking for his presence, but I found nothing again and I also couldn't hear anything. Okay, so the last thing was a little worrying, I thought, throwing my legs over the bed and then putting on my clothes.

As I did that, I couldn't help but feel like I could still feel his hands around my body, touching every part of me.

And I could still remember everything that happened last night and that I was probably going to get pregnant. I had to tell him the good news, I concluded, going out into the hall, looking for him, and then in the kitchen, and my eyes found nothing yet again.

I panicked. I didn't want to admit it, but I was panicking and things were looking worrying. Larry should be around here somewhere, but where that was, I didn't know.

My hands roamed over my belly as if I was already a couple of months pregnant.

That was so silly, I thought, my ears picking up some commotion outside. What was happening there? I asked myself, padding over to the window. I had to make sure that nobody could see me through it, so I was careful, positioning myself behind the wall, and peeking just enough so that I could see what was going on, and I could.

Then, my heart skipped a beat.

I couldn't believe what my eyes were seeing. It was Larry and he was with the police. He wasn't working for them, obviously. They pushed him against the trunk of the police car, making him lie on it. Something clicked. Handcuffs. They were apprehending him, and I really couldn't believe what my eyes were still witnessing.

When did that happen? Was it because he had gone out of the apartment so that he could do something for me? I didn't know, but my mind swirled with thoughts about that, and I just wanted to make sure that he hadn't done anything stupid because of me.

Then, I heard a voice coming from the other side I was hoping I would never have to hear again.

"Larry a.k.a. 'The Rescuer.' You're finally doing something worthwhile with your life, I see."

It was Kenneth. I just couldn't believe it. Not much time had passed since the incident, and I was hoping that he wasn't alive. He was clapping his hands together, and even though I couldn't see his face, I knew he was smirking.

So, it turned out that he was still alive and feeling good enough to be his overconfident self. He was showing off. He thought that he was on top of everything, and now he pretty much was.

Everything regarding me and Larry took a wild turn. Now, I felt how much I wanted to make sure that he was going to be okay, even though it was outside of my influence.

"I'm doing this for Zhaire," Larry stated, spitting onto the ground and showing how much he despised Kenneth.

The latter stopped clapping his hands.

"That's okay. I know you are lying. If she is dead, then where is the body?" He asked, showing me that I wasn't off the hook just yet. He was going to keep looking for me with the police, and I didn't know how to react to that.

What was going on here? I asked myself. Even if I could do anything, it was already too late.

They took Larry inside the police car, closed the door, and that was it. Even if I could do anything to help him right now, it would be pointless. At least, Kenneth went with them, so I didn't have to worry about him possibly finding me here in this apartment, which was a godsend.

I was panting softly, with my back against the wall, and trying to control my breathing as best as I could.

Why did he do that? I had no idea, but it was pretty obvious that he didn't do it because he didn't have a good reason. He did it because he wanted to protect me. The fact that he was going to prison meant that the police and Kenneth, in part, were going to stop looking for me, which was good.

And yet, that all meant I had no idea what I was going to do now.

I still had to tell Larry the good news, though.

CHAPTER 14

Zhaire

It had been months since then, and I was already a couple of months pregnant. My belly was bigger now than it had ever been, and I was living in a different city. I was living in another city, but so many things still felt similar. I was still living in an apartment, and every so often I looked out the windows, checking what was happening outside and making sure that nobody was coming here for me.

I let out a cloud of relief through my nostrils when I realized that the car that was coming down the road wasn't from the police or Kenneth's 'hunting party.'

Even though he had officially stopped looking for me, I knew he was still thinking about me, so that meant that every so often he had people asking questions about me, coming around these parts, trying to sniff me out as best as they could, but it never worked.

If there was something that I learned since all of this started, it was that I knew how to hide well.

This apartment was shitty. It wasn't the kind of place where I wanted to spend a lot of time, and I avoided it as much as I could. Every time that I felt safe enough to go outside, I did.

Trying to remain a little happier about all this, there were a couple of positives about living in this city. It had more green areas, more parks, more places where I could take a walk, and even a free swimming pool for the residents of this apartment building. There wasn't anything special about it, but it was still cool. Not to mention that the people here were also much more friendly than back where I lived.

I took a deep breath, took my purse, and then went outside. I could do this now. I could go and see Larry, and I said I was going to. Ever since that incident where he was sent to jail, he was still serving his sentence. I knew when he would come out, but this whole thing was making me so impatient that I just couldn't wait anymore.

What mattered to me at the moment was going there and seeing him for the first time in months, and then maybe even do something crazy, something that I thought I never would.

Perhaps it was time to settle all of this once and for all.

I was outside, waiting for the cab. It arrived a couple of minutes later, which was unusual. In this city, the people were quite lazy, so I kind of expected the taxi to be late.

I opened the door at the back, sitting down in the backseat. "Where to, my lady?" The taxi driver asked and I gave him the address of the local prison.

He furrowed his brow slightly but still started to drive without saying anything about this, which was relieving. I stared out the window as the taxi continued to drive, heading to my destination. I couldn't and wasn't thinking about anything at the moment. It all felt too surreal.

I couldn't help but wonder if and when I would have to explain to my babies what happened here. I had triplets, so I was going to have to be careful about how I was going to have to approach this subject with them.

For now, it wasn't an issue, I thought, roaming my hands over my belly. I kind of stopped thinking about what was happening around me, not paying much attention to what the driver was saying. Every so often I mumbled something to make sure that he continued chatting and I didn't have to worry about his possible family issues.

Minutes later, when the sun was already in a different position in the sky, I stepped out of the taxi, paid the driver, and then I went inside the prison. I could see the judging looks from the prison guards in the place, but I didn't pay them much attention. I was here for something else, something much more relevant to me.

After giving my name and stating my purpose at the reception desk, I was finally allowed further inside the prison. I crossed several hallways, finally finding myself in the place where I needed to be.

I sat down on the chair, pulling it forward slightly, still feeling my throat dry. I wanted something to drink, but I didn't think they would give me anything. I didn't think that most of the guards in the prison liked me.

Minutes later, the door on the other side finally opened and he stepped inside. His eyes went wide when he realized that I hadn't lied. I was here. Nothing could change that, and I wasn't going anywhere, either.

He sat down on the chair in front of me and a thick, heavy lump formed in my throat. I wanted to reach out through the glass and touch him, feeling his skin again, but I couldn't.

I knew I shouldn't even try doing something like that. I didn't want to risk anything. It was already good enough that the police allowed me to see him and that they found out I didn't have anything to do with that incident that started all this.

After what happened that morning, I had so many questions for him.

"I guess I don't need to say that I am pregnant with your babies," I said and he shook his head slowly.

"You don't need to say anything. I know what happened."

After a moment of silence, I said, "Are you going to tell me why you did what you did?"

"I did it to protect you. Just like I said in the letters I sent to you, I did this to make sure you're going to be safe, and as you can see, it worked. Kenneth and the police stopped looking for you, and now you can live a more fulfilling, happier life – even without me."

I felt a tear coming out. "I can't live without you. I just can't. That's where you are getting it all wrong. I want to be with you.

You are the father of my babies."

He knew that they were triplets, so this was also taking a heavy toll on him. But that was the problem. Larry knowing the truth and everything didn't help.

He always knew everything. He knew what was happening in my life, but he couldn't change it anymore, and now I realized it was getting so difficult not to blame him for all the problems that sprouted out since it all changed for the worse.

"I know that you can't forgive me and I did what I did without your input, but either way, it's too late to do anything about that right now."

What a punch to the gut, and what an asshole he was being right now, just like he was being back then.

CHAPTER 15

Larry

And I was right about that. What I did in the past was in the past and I couldn't change it anymore. I felt good about it, though, and I couldn't do much about that. In the end, I just wanted to make sure that she was going to be okay with my babies. The moment when we made love, I knew she was going to get pregnant, and I didn't do anything about it. I didn't try to stop it. I wanted it to happen, and that was why this all felt like this.

It all felt right and wrong at the same time.

"So, what do you want me to say?" She asked, leaning forward, trying to be closer to me, but she couldn't and that couldn't be changed. When I said that I was going to serve my sentence, I meant it. I wasn't going to try to go back on that, not that I could, anyway.

"You don't need to say anything. If you want to say that you don't love me anymore, that's fine. I just want to make sure that you have everything you need to keep surviving, and when I'm out of here, don't worry – I'll come out seeking you. I will find you."

For a moment, there was only silence again. Her belly was so big. She was still looking at me with surprise and confusion in her eyes. I knew that it was difficult to understand me, so I wasn't so concerned about her reaction.

"I love you, Larry. I don't know how else I can say it, but when I came here, I decided that I didn't want to leave without you."

"What do you mean?" I asked. I didn't know what she was thinking, but what she was suggesting was just impossible. She couldn't take me out of here without me first serving my sentence, and that was the way it was.

"You are the father of my babies. What do you want me to do? Even though it is true that the police don't think anymore that I had anything to do with anything, I'm still always paranoid, and I just can't keep living while knowing that there will be no father for my babies when they finally come."

I opened my mouth, but closed it right away. Zhaire was right about that.

How was I going to be there for my babies when they finally came? I didn't know. I wasn't going to be there, I thought, and at the time, when I had made my decision to give myself up to the police and serve my sentence, I wasn't really thinking straight.

Not as straight as I should've been. I should have thought less about her and more about *us*. About the babies that we would have nine months from then. Gosh, this whole thing was infuriating. I knew that becoming a biker was a mistake. I shouldn't have gone through the whole initiation process, thinking it would all work out.

I wasn't really thinking beyond the fact that I needed to make sure that at least Zhaire was going to come out of this unscathed.

But that wasn't what happened, and I was beginning to think I had been a fool.

But I couldn't think that way about that and not for much longer. It could ruin me, perhaps even making me hate things that didn't have anything to do with this. I loved the fact that I was going to become a biker, but for how long was that going to last and remain unchanged?

"As I said, I want to make sure that you're going to keep living without having to fear that something bad is going to happen to you. I know that things are difficult, but you're going to pull through. I know you will because you are strong. You are the mother of my babies, and when they finally come, I want to be there for them and you as well."

She shook her head, standing up. I knew that she was going to shout through the phone, letting out all of her anger, and I was already bracing myself for it.

"I don't know what you think you're doing. I don't even know what you are thinking is really going to happen in the coming months, but this is all bullshit. You are not being the father I thought you were going to be."

And after that statement, Zhaire thrust the phone back into the cradle and then stormed out of the room, not letting me even say anything that could change her mind, not that I thought there was anything that could be said, anyway.

My body sunk into the chair, my eyes looking at the ceiling after putting my phone back into its respective cradle.

My mind was dizzy with swirling, erratic thoughts. I had no idea what I should do. Zhaire, the mother of my babies, said her piece and this felt like the end of a relationship that was just beginning. Sure, this whole time we had been exchanging letters and talking over the phone when she came here, but that wasn't enough, was it?

And yet, the alternative had been to keep running from the police and Kenneth for who knew how long, and even though that was something I could've done, I didn't want to. I didn't want to do something so stupid, that could have put her life and my babies' lives in danger.

I closed my eyes when I noticed that the prison guard that had come with me here approached me. He was the one charged with making sure that I wasn't going to try to escape.

"Time to go back to your cell, Rescuer," he said, surprising me. I didn't think he knew my nickname from the time when I was a biker.

Everything that had been promised to me from those times wasn't going to happen anymore. Nothing of that existed any longer. I wasn't a biker anymore, and I didn't think I would be that ever again. Right now, I just wanted to make sure that everything was going to be okay with Zhaire and my babies.

So much time had passed that we had even decided on the names for the babies, I remembered, stepping into the hall with the guard and suspecting that he knew more about me than he was letting on.

My babies... Their names were Clinton, Bradley, and Ceyonne. Two baby boys and one baby girl.

I was so happy that I was going to be a father, even though it looked like I wasn't going to be there in the hospital when they finally came.

Or perhaps I was going to be.

Maybe I should do something crazier than all the other things I ever did in my life.

CHAPTER 16

Zhaire

I was possibly doing the worst thing I could be doing. My hand was shaking. I was doing this for myself, for Larry, and also for the babies. But I was going to hurt them, I thought, hating myself for this, but the truth was that there was no way around it.

When Larry said that he wasn't even going to do anything to try and escape from the prison, I was devastated. I didn't even know what to do with myself. I had entered the prison thinking that I was going to get out of there with him, but then he told me he didn't want that, that he wanted to serve his sentence and not be there for my babies when they finally came.

I hated that I was doing this.

But the truth was that ever since that meeting with him, I had become depressed. I was so depressed that every day I had tempting thoughts about killing myself, and I knew I was actually now doing a compromise.

I wasn't going to kill myself, but I was going to get my babies out of me before the birth. My whole body was sweaty. I had no idea if I was even going to survive this, but it was better than nothing.

Outside, everything was happening as it should be. Cars driving on the streets, people walking on the sidewalks, chatting, laughing, cracking jokes, and some sirens echoing in the distance.

Everything was normal, and yet I felt like I was having the

worst mental breakdown of my life. I just couldn't see myself with the babies and alone, especially now that my father had basically given up on me. He said that he didn't want anything to do with me anymore because the marriage that I was going to have with Kenneth wasn't going to happen anymore.

That was why I couldn't help but feel like everything was lost.

I was mustering up enough courage to do it, and just when I was going to do it, the door opened. I had left it open. The door to the living room, which was also the door to my apartment itself.

And in the doorway was none other than Larry himself, and I couldn't believe what my eyes were seeing.

The last thing I thought was going to happen was him showing up here all of a sudden.

He was looking at me with wide eyes. "Zhaire, what are you doing?" He asked, speeding over to me, grabbing my hand, and then forcing me to toss the knife away. I did that, and then I found myself looking at the knife and then at my hand, starting to cry again.

He wrapped me in his arms and I felt the heat of his body and the comfort that it provided me.

I didn't want to be anywhere that wasn't in his arms.

"I was trying to fix everything," I confessed, sobbing in his arms.

"You were trying to hurt my babies. Our babies."

And I couldn't help but wonder what had happened. I was pretty confident that he was still going to be in prison for the next couple of years, so this made no sense.

He wasn't supposed to be here yet. He shouldn't have come out yet. He should still be in prison.

I pushed myself away from him.

There were so many things that he needed to explain, and he was going to explain them to me right now.

"I know, and I hate myself for it. I don't think that I was actually going to go through with it. It's just that after the last time I saw you in prison, I fell into depression, and I started to hate myself, started to hate the world, and started to despise everything around me. And I've missed you so much."

He put his hand on my cheek, caressing it. "I know how much you've missed me, and I'm really sorry for everything that happened, and I'm here to explain everything."

And he'd better explain everything, I thought, pushing myself away from him. Away from his arms.

I was behind the window now and wasn't thinking about going anywhere.

ZHAIRE'S EPILOGUE

"**A**nd you better start explaining everything to me quickly," I barked, letting out a tear. I couldn't stop crying, and I hated myself for it.

"I don't have much time to explain anything. I wasn't actually supposed to come out of prison today."

I turned around quickly, meeting his eyes. "What do you mean that you weren't supposed to come out of prison today? You are here. Everything is fine with you, and…" Just when I was going to continue, I noticed that he still wore his prison garments. They were orange, just like they should be.

"You escaped from prison?" I asked, finding that baffling, covering my mouth with my hand.

"I did. You said that you didn't want to leave the prison without me, and I knew I had to do something about that. I thought about it for a long time, and now I've made my peace with it. This is my life, Zhaire. This is my life with you, and that will never change. I want you to know that."

"But you know what that means. That means that the police are going to come after us again and we are going to have to be on the run. I don't think that I can do that. I will have the babies soon."

"Don't worry, I thought about that, too."

"You thought about that?" I asked, marching toward him and showing my discontentment. I didn't even know what to do with my hands. I just wanted to slap his face and show him how serious I was about this. "Nothing of this makes any sense. What do you think is going to happen now? Do you think that we are all going to have a happy life together and that everything is going to be fine?"

He shook his head. "No, I don't think that is going to happen. Far from that. I think that we are going to have a lot of trouble doing things from this moment onwards, but... this is it. There's no turning back. That's why I said that we need to move fast. The police can't get here while we are still here. If they do, everything that we are doing will be thrown out the window, and in the end, it will all be a waste of time and effort."

I looked at the knife that I had thrown on the floor, thinking that all that I had done before felt like it happened years ago. I supposed that... he was really right. It was just that... thinking that I was going to have to leave everything behind didn't sit right with me, and there was also the fact that we didn't know much about what we would have to do once this was over.

"I don't know what's happening anymore, but I suppose we should get out of here as soon as possible since it's obvious that you just escaped from prison," I said, going into the bedroom, packing my things – as many as I could – and then going out with him and closing the door behind me.

"I'm happy that you are making the right choice. I'm happy that you are sticking with me, but later we are going to have to do something about your depression. I don't want to see you depressed, much less remember that you were almost rejecting our babies. You were going to kill them."

He was right about that. I was so deep into my depression that I didn't want anything that made me remember him, much less his babies.

I just had no idea how I was even going to birth the babies after this, but that was something for another time, something for when we were actually where we could breathe and think about everything that happened.

He had a car. It was parked just outside the apartment building. He opened the door for me, I sat down in the seat, and then he sat down behind the steering wheel.

He turned on the engine and started to drive as fast as he could without pushing through the speed limit.

When we were outside of the city, I said, "I'm so sorry that you had to see me almost killing our babies. I wasn't really going to do it, I promise."

He grabbed my hand, stroking the back of it. "Don't worry about that. I know that you were going through a lot, and I want this to be another beginning for us. It's going to be so much so that we are going to move out of the country. We are going to Mexico. Over there, we can have a good life away from everything happening here, and I'm sure that you are going to love it."

I was looking ahead at the road in front of us. Going to Mexico? I wasn't even going to ask him about how he was going to manage that. There were so many things to consider. Did he even have the fake IDs and passports that we would need to live there without making people suspect that we had secrets we couldn't share with anyone?

I didn't know, but now that we were already doing this, driving outside of the city and proceeding south to Mexico, there was no point in even asking the questions I had in my mind.

I kissed him. It was the only thing that could make me feel better about this, and it also made me feel like everything was going to be fine.

I was sure it was going to be.

LARRY'S EPILOGUE

"I never felt anything for you, and I think you know that," I said. I was talking to the person that was going to become my wife before I came here to Mexico and I realized how much I wanted a change of scenery.

She wasn't crying, but the tone of her voice showed me that she was angry at me. Perhaps she had thought that there was a chance between us, but that was now in the past, and I was here with my wife, who was in the kitchen, behind the stove, preparing something delicious for me.

Her body wasn't as big as it had once been. She had started to lose weight after the pregnancy and delivering the babies.

They were here with me, playing on the carpet in front of me. I was sitting on the couch and watching soccer on TV. It was the most famous sport in the country, and even though I was still beginning to get used to the rules and how they worked, I could tell that I was going to like it.

"You should've told me before about her. I knew something was going on with you, but I didn't think that you were going to keep the truth hidden from me this whole time," she barked.

It was like a punch to my stomach, which was deserving. She had good reasons to hate me, after all.

"I know. I should have told you so many things, but the president... I don't know what was going on with him, but he was really dead set on marrying us, and even though you are nice, you weren't really for me, and I just felt nothing for you."

She took a deep sigh, and I could imagine her shaking her head in disappointment.

"Nothing of that matters anymore. What matters is that I also have found someone I want, someone that is going to make me happy, and he's also a biker just like you. I hope that you're happy, wherever you're living now."

I didn't tell her I was living in Baja California, but that was far from being important right now anyway. I just didn't want any loose ends. I was pretty certain that the police would never come down here looking for me, but in case they got courageous enough to do that, we would be ready.

I was trying to establish a good, fulfilling life with my wife here, but not everything was determined yet. That was why I was paying rent now instead of looking to buy a house, and I would only do that when I had more money, anyway.

"I know, and I'm happy that you've found someone. Goodbye, and good luck," I said.

"Goodbye, Larry," she said, ending the call and leaving me thinking, looking at nothing in particular. I eventually dropped the phone on the seat by my side, checking my babies, who were playing without worrying about anything on the carpet.

They had toys, dolls, and a couple of other things they could play with. They were smiling and having a lot of fun, I could tell.

I stood up slowly, going over to the kitchen. Zhaire was so immersed in what she was doing she didn't even hear me coming. I walked around the kitchen island, wrapping my arms around her slowly from behind.

She melted in my arms, stopping the movement of the spoon that was in one of the pots on the stove. She turned her head slowly around, closing her eyes slightly, her lips looking for mine.

"I heard that you were talking to someone on the phone. Want to tell me who that was?" She probed and I knew she was going to ask me that question. I was already expecting it. If there was something that I had learned about her during this time that we were together, it was that she wanted to know about everything we were doing, including whenever I talked with anyone on the phone.

I guessed that going through the things that she went with me made her paranoid.

"The person that I was going to marry before this all happened."

I was blunt and truthful from the beginning as I was always going to be.

"Her?" She asked, her body suddenly freezing, and then she moved away from me, looking at me with concern in her eyes. "What were you two talking about?"

I took a deep breath in. I didn't want to have to explain everything to her, but since she was my wife now and we were living together, I just had to do it.

"I was telling her a little bit about what happened and I explained that I never felt anything for her. I really never did. You know everything about that part of my life."

She sighed, putting her hands on her waist. "You know, I'm happy that you are here with me and that we have our babies, but still... I don't want to remember anything about my life in America."

I approached her, grabbing her hands and then putting them on my love handles. She loved that, I could tell, examining her eyes.

"I know, and I promise that that was the last time I had to call someone from back over there. It will never happen again."

"You better promise me that again. I want to make sure that you mean it."

I leaned my head down to hers, looking deeply into her eyes.

"I promise it. I promise that it won't happen again and that this is really the beginning you want for us."

And having said that, I moved my hand up, cupping the nape of her neck. And we kissed again and it was as sweet as all the other times we kissed, but there was also something different about it.

Something deeper. Stronger.

It was our love for each other.

The End

Looking for the first two books in the series? You can find them here:

1. Biker's Lost Baby
2. Biker's Secret Twins

And, leave your review. Your feedback helps me improve a lot!

TEASER: BIKER'S SECRET TWINS

BWWM Dark Mafia Romance

I had no idea what I was doing. Someone like him was obviously off-limits, and yet I kept on thinking that something was going to happen between us. Why did I think that? Because he was absolutely, undoubtedly smoking hot, and just looking at him was enough to make me feel some wetness in my pussy.

He was standing in front of me, and he was so close that I could almost smell the breath coming out of his mouth.

He had me cornered against the wall, and I couldn't move, couldn't go anywhere. My boyfriend could see me doing this, and he would be pissed. He would be so angry that the first thing he would do would be to pull out his gun and shoot at this handsome man standing in front of me.

He looked like the opposite of a star. He was rugged, a little dirty, rough, and muscular, and he had thick, dense hair on his chest, which was one of the things about him that most stood out. I couldn't stop looking down and... admiring it. It just made my nipples so hard.

It made me feel increased wetness in my pussy, and I soon found myself pressing my legs together, as though I was afraid that he was going to impale himself between them if I wasn't doing it.

I knew that it was a silly thought, especially because he would never do anything to me that I didn't want. Even though I had an okay relationship with my boyfriend, recently he had begun to show me that he didn't care much about me.

He didn't care much about my issues, and this man standing right here, holding the beer can in his hand, was beginning to show me that he was so much better.

So much more like a real man.

He was taller than me, so much so that I could imagine myself putting my arms around his body and letting him put his chin on top of my head, something I was certain he was also thinking about.

"Someone like you shouldn't have been left alone like this. A man like me might steal you," he threatened, making me hate him more than I already did.

It didn't matter how hot he was, he was always going to make me feel irritated with his snarky comments. He was always so assured of himself, and that was something that would never change.

My body was beginning to get hotter. I had to do something about it, but I couldn't. Again, I remembered that he had me cornered against the wall.

I could only hear the pounding music coming from behind me, reminding me that the party was still going strong.

"I'm not going to let you do that. It doesn't matter how hot, how important, how smart, and how pretty much everything else you think you are, you are not going to make me cheat on my boyfriend."

"Is that so?" He asked, brushing his finger on my cheek, and I could almost feel myself physically recoiling, but I didn't do it because I didn't want to show weakness, especially not in front of someone with such a high opinion of himself.

"That's right. It's something that you can't change about us, and you need to start to get used to it."

He curled up the right corner of his lips. "You are always trying to be so tough, but in the end, you are nothing more than a girl that needs to shut up and do exactly everything I want. I'm above your boyfriend when it comes to pretty much everything, and that's also something that will never be changed."

"I don't care. I'm with James and that's everything that matters," I tried to say, trying to push him away with my hand, but it didn't work. Fred didn't budge. I knew that he wasn't going to, especially after emptying a few beer cans.

He wasn't drunk, but he was still totally unhinged. He was much bolder right now, to the point of brushing his fingers on my cheek, which he was doing again.

I lifted my hand. I was going to slap his face to show him that I wasn't kidding. Not to mention that he should be feeling ashamed of himself. What the hell was he thinking could even happen between us that wouldn't usher a catastrophe to the motorcycle club? Was he thinking about fully destroying it, especially after everything that happened under Harry's leadership?

He was the former president of the biker club and also its founder. He was the one that established everything, but now he was living far away from the country. It was Fred, a.k.a. 'Promise', that had picked up the pieces and melded them together.

It meant that the motorcycle club was 'back in shape' but it was still far from enough to instill fear in the other motorcycle club members, something I was sure that he didn't like one bit.

Having drunk a little tonight, I was also beginning to feel that I was a little unhinged. I mean, what was I even thinking was going to happen between us? I didn't know, but standing here in the middle of this hallway, where everybody could see us, just wasn't doing me any favors, and I was beginning to grow paranoid that my whole life was going to be ruined.

It was with that thought in mind that I stated incisively, "You need to leave. I need to go back to my boyfriend, go back to James, and we need to pretend that this never happened."

And this time, I could feel my rage bubbling in my veins. I just wanted to punch his face until he was asking for my forgiveness, but I knew how pointless that would be, especially because he was so much stronger than me. Not to mention that he was growing bolder as time passed, and I knew he was about to do something stupid.

I could see him lowering his head.

I couldn't do anything about it, especially when our lips finally connected. I knew that I should be slapping his face until he was recoiling away from me, but that was so difficult, especially when his lips were so sweet. So good. So tender, and the kiss was a lot more than I thought it would be.

There was no denying that Fred was a good kisser.

SIMILAR BOOKS

SERIES - ALPHA HUNTERS

1. Not my Wedding
2. Not my Vows
3. Not his Baby
4. Not my Fiancé
5. Not my Daughter

SERIES - RUTHLESS MAFIOSOS

1. His Accidental Triplets
2. His Sweet Captive
3. His Stolen Bride
4. His Accidental Baby
5. His Secret Triplets
6. His Fleeing Single Mom
7. Not my Daughter
8. Not my Fiancé

ABOUT THE AUTHOR

Ruthless mafiosos, gorgeous billionaires, and feisty heroines are just tiny fractions of Jolie Damman's stories. She breathes and lives dark romance, peppering each scene with intrigue and tension that sweep readers away.

When she isn't writing, she's reading by the fireplace of her house as she takes sips of her tea.

www.ingramcontent.com/pod-product-compliance
Lightning Source LLC
Chambersburg PA
CBHW051454150726
48000CB00005B/2396